Waiting for the Whales

Sheryl McFarlane

Illustrated by Ron Lightburn

Philomel Books

Once, in a cedar-shingled cottage on a bluff by the sea, there lived an old man.

In the evenings, he looked out over the water, shimmering with the last rays of light. Often he saw bald eagles soaring, majestic herons fishing, and fat seals lounging on the rocky island that would disappear at high tide.

But it was the orcas he longed to see. They traveled up and down the strait in front of his home. Sometimes he caught sight of them blowing in the distance. They were so very far away that seeing them only made him lonely.

Every summer, the whales came in close to shore. They rubbed their enormous backs against the rocks of the island. And they feasted on salmon bound for spawning grounds up the creek that ran past the old man's garden into the sea.

The old man watched the pod of orcas leap and breach and smack their tail flukes against the water. And as he stood on the bluff, his heart leapt with the whales below. To him, there was nothing more wonderful than these great mammals of the sea.

Each fall as the whales departed, tears filled his eyes. He was alone again.

Even though his children had long since moved away, the old man continued to grow a huge garden, an enormous garden, a gigantic garden.

He tilled and he planted. He weeded and he watered. And when the crop was ready, he gave most of it away.

He was just one old man, and he couldn't eat everything he grew.

Sometimes during the long winter months, he collected oysters from the island that he could walk to at low tide. Or he dug clams on the sand spit. After each storm, which shook the great firs and bent the giant cedars up and down the coast, he collected seaweed for his garden.

Other times he walked in the nearby woods, watched over by the jagged peaks of the coastal range. He loved these woods. He had worked in them his whole life, and they had been his playground as a child long, long ago.

He knew each tree, each clearing, each trail and where it led.

He knew where to collect the best salal to send to florist shops in the city.

He knew where to gather watercress for his soups.

And he was always on the lookout for fallen logs, which could be sawed up for firewood to keep the chill of winter from his old bones.

But sometimes he stared out at the fish boats that bobbed on the misty gray water and waited for the orcas to return.

One crisp spring day, the old man's daughter arrived unexpectedly. In one arm she held her bags, and in the other, a tiny baby girl.

The old man grumbled something about noisy babies. But as he held the tiny infant, he remembered holding his own children when they were small.

When he spotted the orcas that summer, he carried his granddaughter to the water's edge and held her up so she could see. And although he knew she didn't understand, he told her all about the whales that he had watched since he was small.

The tiny baby girl grew into a serious little girl, a wild little girl, a stubborn little girl.

She stuck to her grandfather like glue. And although he grumbled about it, he took her everywhere.

In the garden, they tilled and they planted. They weeded and they watered.

And when the crop was ready, they gave most of it away (except for the raspberries, which the little girl loved best of all).

Sometimes during the long winter months, they collected oysters or dug clams. And after each storm, they gathered seaweed for the garden.

Other times they walked in the woods. The little girl learned each tree, each clearing, each trail and where it led. She learned where to find the best salal patches and where to gather watercress for soups.

She learned to look for fallen logs, which could be sawed into firewood to keep the chill of winter from her grandfather's old bones.

In the evenings, they watched the tugs with loaded barges inch down the coast. But it was the orcas that they waited for.

Then one spring, the old man refused to till or to plant, to water or to weed. "It's time for me to rest" was all he said.

That year, mother and daughter tilled and planted the garden. They watered and they weeded, and when the crop was ready, they gave most of it away. They gathered salal and watercress and brought in the wood to keep the chill of winter from their bones.

The old man helped them sometimes. But usually he sat on the porch in front of his cedar-shingled cottage on the bluff by the sea.

He saw bald eagles soaring, majestic herons fishing, and fat seals lounging on the rocky island that would disappear at high tide. Each night as he looked out over the water, shimmering with the last rays of light, he waited for the orcas to return.

The day the orcas came that summer, the old man died.

And when the little girl wept for her grandfather, her mother dried her tears. "Don't be sad, sweet girl. Your grandfather's spirit has gone to leap and swim with the whales."

Many times that winter, mother and daughter looked out over the stormy gray water of the strait, waiting for the orcas to return.

One hot evening in July, the girl's mother sent her to water the garden. Before she turned to climb the hill back to the house, she looked out toward the island. She saw them. Orcas. Powerful flashes against the warm glow of golden water. But something was different. She sensed it right away. Some of the whales seemed to be hanging back.

Moments later, the bay was filled with black dorsal fins cutting through the water. When the girl spotted a calf swimming between its mother and an old bull, a fierce cry of joy escaped her.

And right away, she flew up the hill to tell her mother.

To the bond between young and old; in memory of Roy Padgett;
and in memory of my own grandfather, who lives still in my heart.
With special thanks to my husband and family;
and to my editor, Ann Featherstone, for her insight and tact.—S.M.

To Sam, with love.
Thanks to Bill, Allison, Devon, and
Andrea and a tip of the hat to Claire.—R.L.

First American Edition published in 1993 by Philomel Books, a division of
The Putnam & Grosset Group, 200 Madison Avenue, New York, NY 10016.
Originally published in 1991 by Orca Book Publishers, Victoria. Printed in Hong Kong.
Book design by Colleen Flis.

Library of Congress Cataloging-in-Publication Data
McFarlane, Sheryl. Waiting for the whales / Sheryl McFarlane ;
illustrated by Ron Lightburn.   p.   cm.
Summary: A lonely old man who waits each year to see the orcas
swim past his house imparts his love of the whales to his granddaughter.
[1. Killer whale—Fiction. 2. Whales—Fiction. 3. Grandfathers—
Fiction. 4. Death—Fiction] I. Lightburn, Ron, ill. II. Title.
PZ7.M478462Wai 1993 [E]—dc20 92-25117 CIP AC
ISBN 0-399-22515-3

1 3 5 7 9 10 8 6 4 2
First American Edition